W9-DEH-776

Big Green Crocodile

by Jay Dale
illustrated by Anna Hancock

Min Monkey ran down
to the river.
Grandpa Tut came, too.

"Come back! Come back, you silly little monkey!" shouted Grandpa Tut. "Big Green Crocodile is down by the river. She is hiding from you in the long brown reeds!"

4

"I cannot see
Big Green Crocodile,"
said Min Monkey.
"I will **not** come back to you.
I am playing with my friends."

Splash!

Min Monkey was having
lots of fun with his friends.

Swish!

"Help! Help!" cried Min Monkey.
"Who is in the long brown reeds?
Is it Big Green Crocodile?"

"Yes!" shouted Grandpa Tut.
"Get out of the river,
you silly little monkey."

11

Min Monkey ran up
and into the big tree.
All Min Monkey's friends ran up
and into the big tree, too.

Min Monkey saw the reeds
go this way and that.

Swish! Swish! Swish!

"Oh, no!" cried Min Monkey.
"Big Green Crocodile
is coming out of the reeds!"

Ribbit!

Ribbit!

"Look!" said Min Monkey.
"A little green frog
is coming out of the reeds!"
Then . . .

Big Green Crocodile
came out of the reeds, too!